NO LONGER THE PROPERTY OF
THE SALEM PUBLIC LIBRARY

PowerKids Readers:
The Bilingual Library of the United States of America™

Bilingual Edition
English/Spanish
Edición bilingüe

OKLAHOMA

VANESSA BROWN

TRADUCCIÓN AL ESPAÑOL: MARÍA CRISTINA BRUSCA

The Rosen Publishing Group's
PowerKids Press™ & **Editorial Buenas Letras**™
New York

Published in 2006 by The Rosen Publishing Group, Inc.
29 East 21st Street, New York, NY 10010

Copyright © 2006 by The Rosen Publishing Group, Inc.

All rights reserved. No part of this book may be reproduced in any form without permission in writing from the publisher, except by a reviewer.

First Edition

Book Design: Albert B. Hanner
Photo Credits: Cover © Richard Hamilton Smith/Corbis; p. 5 Albert B. Hanner; p. 7 © 2002 Geoatlas; pp. 9, 30 (State Nickname), 31 (spring) © David Muench/Corbis; pp. 11, 17, 31 (Rogers), (Thorpe), (Albert), (Tallchief), (Mantle) © Bettmann/Corbis; p. 13, 31 (territory) © Corbis; p. 15 © Burstein Collection/Corbis; pp. 19, 30 (State motto) © Peter Turnley/Corbis; p. 21 © Ed Blochowak/Associated Press, The Shawnee News-Star; p. 23 © Jeff Albertson/Corbis; pp. 25, 30 (Capital) © Denny Lehman/Corbis; p. 30 (State Flower) © Clay Perry/Corbis, (State Bird) © Tim Zurowski/Corbis, (State Tree) © Raymond Gehman/Corbis; p. 31 (Brooks) © Michael Gerber/Corbis

Library of Congress Cataloging-in-Publication Data

Brown, Vanessa, 1963–
Oklahoma / Vanessa Brown ; traducción al español, María Cristina Brusca. — 1st ed.
p. cm. — (The bilingual library of the United States of America) Includes bibliographical references and index.
ISBN 1-4042-3101-3 (library binding)
1. Oklahoma—Juvenile literature. I. Title. II. Series.
F694.3.B76 2006
976.6-dc22
2005020507

Manufactured in the United States of America

Due to the changing nature of Internet links, Editorial Buenas Letras has developed an online list of Web sites related to the subject of this book. This site is updated regularly. Please use this link to access the list:

http://www.buenasletraslinks.com/ls/oklahoma

Contents

1. Welcome to Oklahoma ... 4
2. Oklahoma Geography ... 6
3. Oklahoma History ... 10
4. Living in Oklahoma ... 18
5. Oklahoma Today ... 22
6. Let´s Draw a Native American Hut ... 26
   Timeline/Oklahoma Events ... 28–29
   Oklahoma Facts ... 30
   Famous Oklahomans/Words to Know ... 31
   Resources/Word Count/Index ... 32

Contenido

1. Bienvenidos a Oklahoma ... 4
2. Geografía de Oklahoma ... 6
3. Historia de Oklahoma ... 10
4. La vida en Oklahoma ... 18
5. Oklahoma, hoy ... 22
6. Dibujemos una choza nativoamericana ... 26
   Cronología/ Eventos en Oklahoma ... 28–29
   Datos sobre Oklahoma ... 30
   Oklahomenses famosos/ Palabras que debes saber ... 31
   Recursos/ Número de palabras/ Índice ... 32

Welcome to Oklahoma

These are the flag and the seal of the state of Oklahoma. Oklahoma got its name from Native American words. In the language of the Choctaw, *okla* means "people." *Homa* means "red."

Bienvenidos a Oklahoma

Estos son la bandera y el escudo de Oklahoma. Oklahoma tomó su nombre de palabras nativoamericanas. En el idioma choctaw, *okla* quiere decir "gente" y *homa* significa "rojo."

Oklahoma Flag and State Seal

Bandera y escudo de Oklahoma

Oklahoma Geography

Oklahoma borders the states of Colorado, Kansas, Texas, Missouri, New Mexico, and Arkansas. Because of its shape, the northwest part of the state is known as the Panhandle.

Geografía de Oklahoma

Oklahoma linda con los estados de Colorado, Kansas, Texas, Misuri, Nuevo México y Arkansas. Debido a su forma, la región noroeste del estado es conocida como el *panhandle*, o agarradera de sartén.

Map of Oklahoma

Mapa de Oklahoma

COLORADO
KANSAS
MISSOURI / MISURI
New Mexico / Nuevo México
TEXAS
ARKANSAS

OKLAHOMA

- Guymon
- Woodward
- Elk City
- ★ Oklahoma City
- Tulsa
- Broken Arrow
- Ardmore
- Durant

Rivers:
- Cimarron River / Río Cimarrón
- Arkansas River / Río Arkansas
- Canadian River / Río Canadian
- Red River / Río Red

Map Key
Claves del mapa

- ○ Major City / Ciudad principal
- ★ Capital / Capital
- ～ River / Río

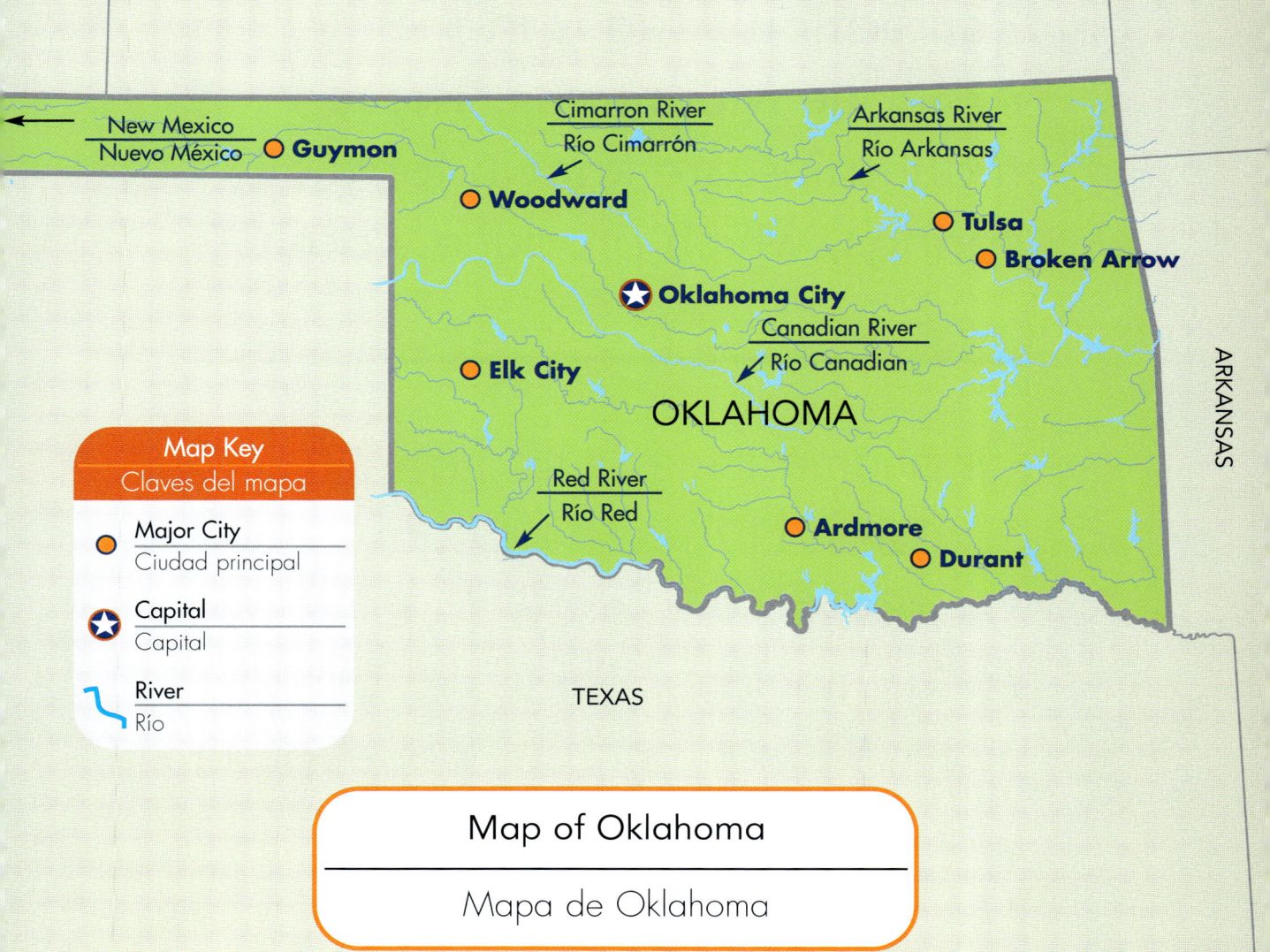

Oklahoma has 50 state parks. The Chickasaw National Recreation Area is in the Arbuckle Mountains. These mountains are known for their springs, which produce water.

Oklahoma tiene 50 parques estatales. El Área Nacional Recreativa Chickasaw se encuentra en las montañas Arbuckle. Estas montañas son famosas por el agua que surge de sus manantiales.

Chickasaw National Recreation Area

Área Nacional Recreativa Chickasaw

Oklahoma History

In 1541, Spanish explorer Francisco Vásquez de Coronado became the first European to reach Oklahoma. Coronado was looking for a city of gold. This city did not exist.

Historia de Oklahoma

En 1541, el explorador español Francisco Vásquez de Coronado fue el primer europeo en llegar a Oklahoma. Coronado buscaba una ciudad de oro. Esta ciudad no existía.

Explorer Francisco Vásquez de Coronado

Explorador Francisco Vásquez de Coronado

In the 1820s, the U.S. government forced Native American groups into an area called Indian Territory. This territory is present-day Oklahoma. Oklahoma is the home of more than 67 Native American groups.

En la década de 1820, el gobierno de los E.U.A. obligó a muchos grupos nativoamericanos a trasladarse a un área llamada Territorio Indio. En esta tierra se encuentra hoy Oklahoma. En Oklahoma viven más de 67 grupos nativoamericanos.

Ponch Indians Gather for the Sun Dance in Oklahoma

Danza de la tribu Ponch dedicada al sol, en Oklahoma

Sequoyah was a Cherokee who lived in Oklahoma. Sequoyah wanted to find a way to write the Cherokee language. Back then Cherokee was only spoken. He created the Cherokee alphabet.

Sequoya fue un cheroqui que vivió en Oklahoma. Sequoya quería hallar una forma de escribir el idioma cheroqui. En esos días el cheroqui era solamente hablado. Sequoya creó el alfabeto de la lengua cheroqui.

Sequoyah and His Cherokee Alphabet

Sequoya y su alfabeto cheroqui

In the 1930s, Oklahoma suffered from lack of water and sandstorms. These years are known as the Dust Bowl years. Fields were dry and cattle died. These were very hard times for Oklahomans.

En la década de 1930, Oklahoma sufrió grandes sequías y tormentas de polvo. Esta época se conoce como los años de la Gran Tormenta de Polvo. Los campos se secaron y el ganado se murió. Fue un tiempo muy difícil para Oklahoma.

Dust Storm in Guymon, Oklahoma, 1937

Tormenta de polvo en Guymon, Oklahoma, en 1937

Living in Oklahoma

The Red Earth Native American Festival takes place in Oklahoma City. The festival honors the music, dance, and food of Native Americans.

La vida en Oklahoma

El Festival Nativoamericano de la Tierra Roja tiene lugar en Oklahoma City. Este festival honra la música, danza y comida de los pueblos nativoamericanos.

Native North American at the Red Earth Festival

Nativo norteamericano en el Festival de la Tierra Roja

Rodeos are very popular in Oklahoma. More than 100 rodeos take place in the state every year. The International Finals Rodeo in Oklahoma City is the largest rodeo in Oklahoma.

Los rodeos son muy populares en Oklahoma. Cada año se realizan más de 100 rodeos en el estado. El Rodeo Internacional en Oklahoma City es el rodeo más grande de Oklahoma.

A Rodeo in Oklahoma

Rodeo en Oklahoma

Oklahoma Today

The Oklahoma City National Memorial opened in 2000. It honors the people who died in the bombing of a government building in April 1995. The bomb killed 168 people.

Oklahoma, hoy

El Monumento Nacional a Oklahoma City se inauguró en el año 2000. Está dedicado a las personas que murieron en una explosión en un edificio del gobierno en abril de 1995. 168 personas murieron al explotar una bomba.

The Oklahoma City National Memorial

Monumento Nacional a Oklahoma City

Oklahoma City, Tulsa, Lawton, and Norman are important cities in Oklahoma. Oklahoma City is the capital of the state.

Oklahoma City, Tulsa, Lawton y Norman son ciudades importantes de Oklahoma. Oklahoma City es la capital del estado.

State Capitol in Oklahoma City

Capitolio del estado en Oklahoma City

Activity:
Let´s draw a Native American hut

Actividad:
Dibujemos una choza nativoamericana

1

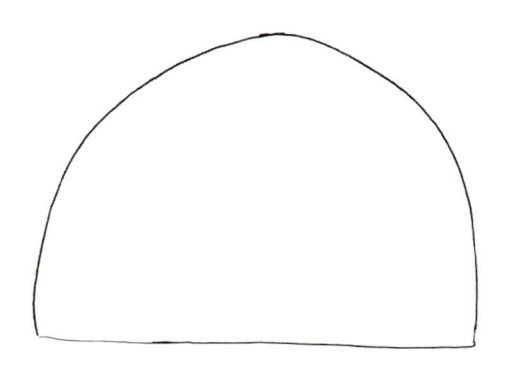

First draw a dome, or half-circle shape.

Comienza por dibujar una cúpula o forma semicircular.

2

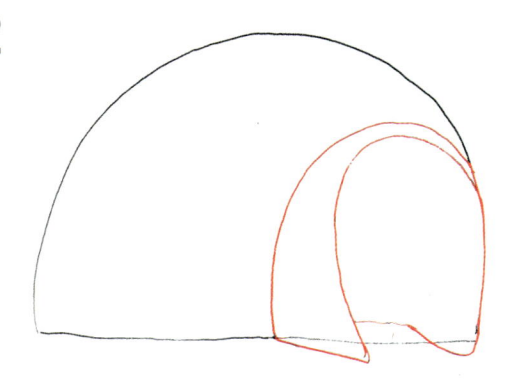

Add a horseshoe shape for the door.

Agrega una forma de herradura para dibujar la puerta.

3

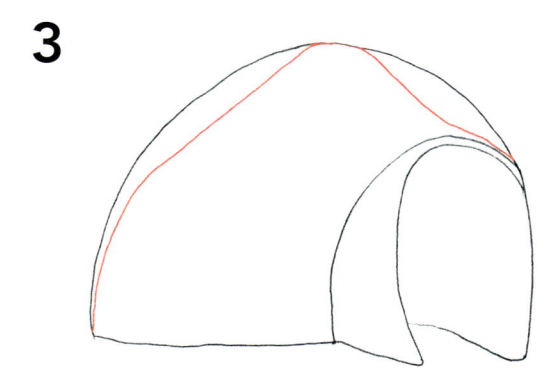

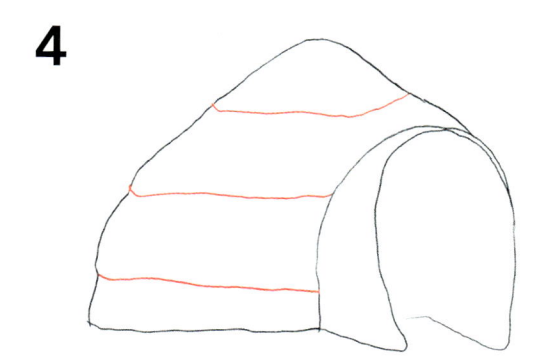

Erase extra lines. Draw the top of the hut.

Borra las líneas sobrantes. Traza la forma de la parte superior. Borra ahora las líneas de guía.

4

Erase extra lines. Separate the hut into pieces using curved horizontal lines.

Borra ahora las líneas de guía. Divide la choza en varias partes trazando líneas curvas horizontales.

5

Shade the hut by drawing short vertical lines. Keep the three horizontal lines in white. These are the ropes that hold the sticks to the hut.

Sombrea la choza con trazos verticales cortos. Deja las líneas horizontales en blanco. Éstas son las cuerdas que atan las ramitas a la choza.

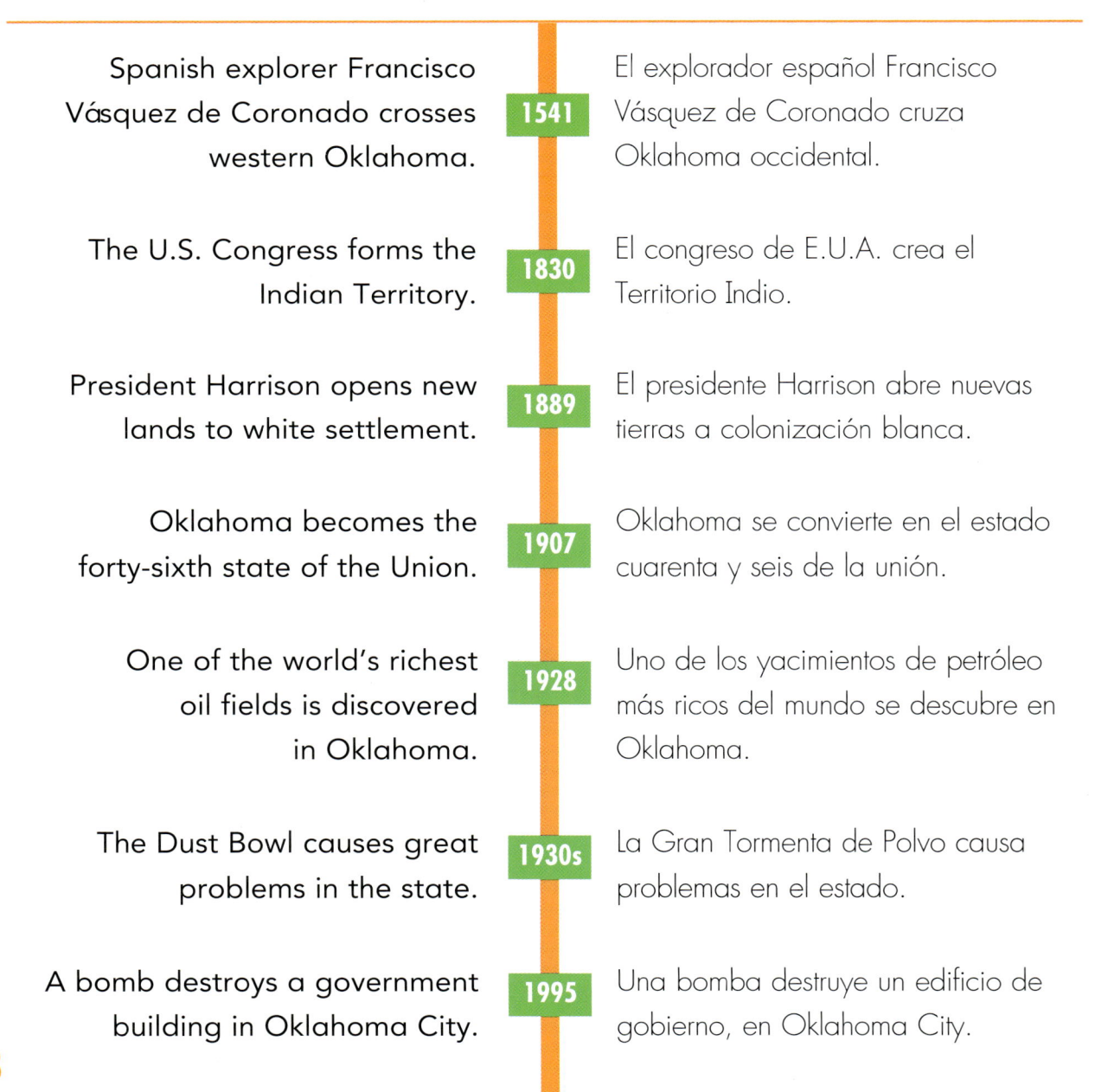

Timeline / Cronología

1541 — Spanish explorer Francisco Vásquez de Coronado crosses western Oklahoma. / El explorador español Francisco Vásquez de Coronado cruza Oklahoma occidental.

1830 — The U.S. Congress forms the Indian Territory. / El congreso de E.U.A. crea el Territorio Indio.

1889 — President Harrison opens new lands to white settlement. / El presidente Harrison abre nuevas tierras a colonización blanca.

1907 — Oklahoma becomes the forty-sixth state of the Union. / Oklahoma se convierte en el estado cuarenta y seis de la unión.

1928 — One of the world's richest oil fields is discovered in Oklahoma. / Uno de los yacimientos de petróleo más ricos del mundo se descubre en Oklahoma.

1930s — The Dust Bowl causes great problems in the state. / La Gran Tormenta de Polvo causa problemas en el estado.

1995 — A bomb destroys a government building in Oklahoma City. / Una bomba destruye un edificio de gobierno, en Oklahoma City.

Oklahoma Events

February
Chocolate Festival in Norman

April
Azalea Festival in Muskogee
Festival of the Arts in Oklahoma City
International Finals Rodeo in Oklahoma City

May
Strawberry Festival in Stilwell

June
Red Earth Festival in Bartlesville, in Oklahoma City

August – September
State Fair in Oklahoma City

November
Cheese Festival in Watonga

December
Territorial Christmas Celebration in Guthrie

Eventos en Oklahoma

Febrero
Festival del chocolate, en Norman

Abril
Festival de la azalea, en Muskogee
Festival de las artes, en Oklahoma City
Finales Internacionales de Rodeo, en Oklahoma City

Mayo
Festival de la fresa, en Stilwell

Junio
Festival de la Tierra Roja, en Bartlesville, en Oklahoma City

Agosto – Septiembre
Feria del estado, en Oklahoma City

Noviembre
Festival del queso, en Watonga

Diciembre
Celebración territorial de la Navidad, en Guthrie

Oklahoma Facts/Datos sobre Oklahoma

Population 3.4 million		Población 3.4 millones
Capital Oklahoma City		Capital Oklahoma City
State Motto Labor Conquers All Things		Lema del estado El trabajo todo lo puede
State Flower Mistletoe		Flor del estado Muérdago
State Bird Scissor-tailed Flycatcher		Ave del estado Tijereta
State Nickname The Sooner State		Mote del estado El Estado Pronto
State Tree Redbud		Árbol del estado Ciclamor
State Song "Oklahoma"		Canción del estado "Oklahoma"

Famous Oklahomans/Oklahomenses famosos

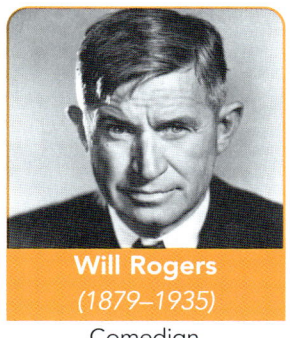

Will Rogers
(1879–1935)
Comedian
Comediante

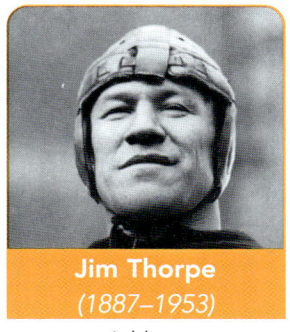

Jim Thorpe
(1887–1953)
Athlete
Atleta

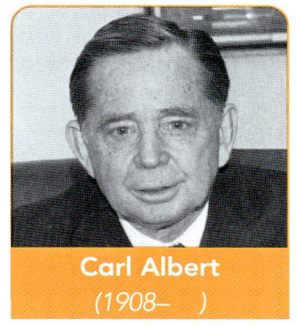

Carl Albert
(1908–   )
Politician
Político

Maria Tallchief
(1925–   )
Ballerina
Bailarina

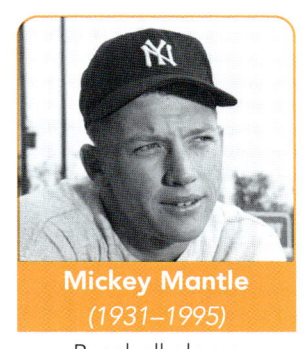

Mickey Mantle
(1931–1995)
Baseball player
Jugador de béisbol

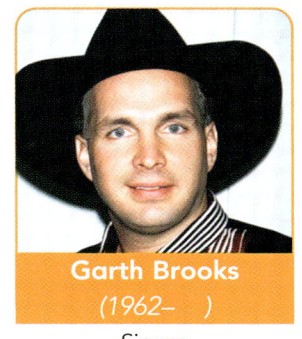

Garth Brooks
(1962–   )
Singer
Cantante

Words to Know/Palabras que debes saber

border
frontera

panhandle
agarradera de sartén

spring
manantial

territory
territorio

31

Here are more books to read about Oklahoma:
Otros libros que puedes leer sobre Oklahoma:

In English/En inglés:

Oklahoma
America the Beautiful
by Reedy, Jerry and Heinrichs, Anne
Children's Press, 1998

My First Book About Oklahoma
The Oklahoma Experience
by Marsh, Carol
Gallopade International, 2000

Words in English: 315

Palabras en español: 323

Index

A
Arbuckle Mountains, 8

B
borders, 6

C
Cherokee language, 14
Chickasaw National Recreation Area, 8

Choctaw Nation, 7
Coronado, Francisco Vásquez de, 10

D
Dust Bowl, 16

F
flag, 22

O
Oklahoma City Memorial, 22

P
Panhandle, 6

S
Sequoyah, 24

Índice

A
agarradera, 6
Area Nacional Recreativa Chickasaw, 8

C
Coronado, Francisco Vásquez de, 10

F
fronteras, 6

G
Gran Tormenta de Polvo, 16

I
idioma cheroqui, 14

M
montañas Arbuckle, 8
Monumento Nacional a Oklahoma City, 22

N
pueblo chocktaw, 7

S
Sequoya, 24